Harriet Jane Hanson Robinson

Captain Mary Miller

A drama

Harriet Jane Hanson Robinson

Captain Mary Miller
A drama

ISBN/EAN: 9783337083298

Printed in Europe, USA, Canada, Australia, Japan

Cover: Foto ©Andreas Hilbeck / pixelio.de

More available books at **www.hansebooks.com**

𝔄 𝔇𝔯𝔞𝔪𝔞

BY

HARRIET H. ROBINSON.

"But, if you ask me what offices women may fill, I reply — any.
I do not care what case you put; let them be sea-captains if you
will." — MARGARET FULLER (in 1844).

BOSTON:

Walter H. Baker & Co.

CHARACTERS:

NATHAN GANDY . . . . *A retired sea-captain.*

WILLIAM MILLER . . *A down-East skipper, afterwards captain of the Creole Bride.*

MR. ROMBERG . . . . *A ship-owner.*

HANK (or Henry) MUDGETT . . . . *The cook, a Nantucket boy.*

PATSY HEFRON . . . . *Mate of the Creole Bride.*

JOSEPHUS HERODOTUS, called PHUS * . . *The Captain's boy.*

LORANY GANDY . . . . *Wife of Captain Gandy.*

MARY GANDY . . . . . *Daughter of Capt. and Mrs. Gandy.*

LEAFY JANE GANDY . . } *Children of Capt. and Mrs. Gandy.*
JOHN QUINCY ADAMS GANDY }

* This part may be changed to that of a girl, named PHUSEPHONY (PERSEPHONE) HERODIAS.

CAPTAIN MARY MILLER.

ACT I.

NATHAN GANDY'S *house, near the wharf in Annisport.*
Living-room. Fireplace, R. *Doors,* R. *and* L. *and back.*
Table, R. C., *on which is a braided-rag mat, partly done.*
Chairs, pictures of ships. a mourning piece (weeping wil-
low hanging over a tomb) MRS. GANDY *with a broom.*
She sweeps carefully away from the middle of the room.

MRS. G. There! there's that plaguy money for me to
sweep raound agin! I'm tired to death on it, I be; an' that's a
fac', I can't half sweep my floor! But, I snum, I won't pick
it up! I told Nathan I wouldn't, an' I won't!

    (*Enter* CAPTAIN GANDY, L., *singing.*)

> " On Springfield's maountins there did dwell
> A lovelye youth, an' known full well,
> Leftenant Carter's onlie son,
> A galliant youth, nigh twenty-one."

    (*Sees his wife, who does not look up.*)

CAPT. G. Hullo, Lorany! didn't know yer was thar.
What makes yer so glum? (*Aside*) Oh, the caarf, I bet!
Say, Lorany, I'm plaguy sorry I sold the caarf. I'd buy her
back, but the fellers 'd laf at me. I told some on 'em haow
bad yer felt, daown to the store. And old Pete Rosson, he was
a-sittin' on a kintle o' salt fish; he said: "Wimmin's rights! I
s'pose Mis' Gandy went ter the meetin' and heerd the lectur'-
woman. I guess Mis' Rosson wouldn't dare ter complain

3

ef I sold one o' her caarfs. I'd let her know they was *mine*, double quick." Won't yer take up yer money, Lorany?

MRS. G. (*dusting*). No! Nathan, I won't! So, there! It 'ill hev to stay there, wher' it dropped, for all o' me; for I'll never pick it up as long as I live. I tho't all we had was aourn together, and that everything belonged as much ter me as it does ter you. But I see naow that it's as the lectur'-woman sed. I read it in the *Transkip:*—"Husband and wife is one, but that one is the husband." I shouldn't 'a' tho't o' sellin' yaour caarf or yaour best caow. You call 'em yaourn, an' the caarf was allus called mine. An', then, little Sally, that's gone, tho't so much on't! (*Wipes her eyes.*)

CAPT. G. Hang it! don't take on so. (*Aside*) Darn them fellers, flingin' their wimmin's right at me! (*To her*) Who cares what the lectur'-woman says? Some darned old maid, or divorced widder, I s'pose. Didn't I buy suthin' for yer with the money! Didn't I buy yer a gaown, a shawl, an' a bun-nit! An', when yer didn't like 'em, didn't I give yer all the money back, and yer wouldn't take it! An' didn't yer fling it daown on the floor, an' vaow you wouldn't pick it up!

MRS. G. Yes, but yer never as'd me! an' I didn't want her sold, nuther! You know haow I took care o' that caarf. Her mother died, an' never saw her. I almost feel as if she was mine; for I brought her up like a baby, and she sucked milk from my finger before she could stan'. I'm sure I'm as much her mother as harf the hens are mothers of their chickens: for they never see some o' the eggs till they are put under 'em to hatch, an' they don't know which is which.

CAPT. G. Waal! yaou've got yer new things, hain't ye? an' I'm glad on't. I'm abaout sick o' them black clo'es o' yourn. They look so maugre. For my part, I want ter see yer in suthin' bright.

MRS. G. I sh'd think yer did! Yer tho't I was abaout sixteen, didn't yer? (*Opens the door at the back, and produces a very showy piece of dress goods, a shawl of a very loud pattern, and a bonnet trimmed with green and red and yellow*) Look a' that! What do you think o' them things!

Young enough for Mary, or Leafy Jane, either. I never wore such bright things when I was a gal; an' I'm sure I ain't a-gwine ter begin naow.

CAPT. G. I don't see why, Lorany! They ain't no brighter than the marygoolds, pecuniaries (*petunias*), and dadyoluses, yer like so well, in the garden, or even the per-salter roses.

MRS. G. That's a different thing. I ain't a flower-garden; I do wish the men-folks 'd let their wives buy their own clo'es, or give 'em the money to buy 'em with. (*Sits down and braids on her mat.*)

CAPT. G. Why, Lorany! the wimmen folks ain't used to layin' out money. We can make it spend a great deal better 'n they can.

MRS. G. P'r'aps yer can; but we'd like what we bought ourselves a great deal better; I do wish they'd let us buy our own clo'es, I say, or give us the money to buy 'em with, so's we could suit ourselves.

CAPT. G. Wall, I snum, yer as bad as the lectur'-woman Pete Rosson told on. He said she said wimmen ort-ter have their own private pusses, same's the men, and other things tew; and that the Legislater ort to see tew't, but that they was tew busy, — trying to settle the size of a bar'l o' cramberries, an' talkin' baout sellin' eggs by weight, and sich things, — to care what becomes o' wimmin's rights. Sellin' eggs by weight! what durned nonsense! Some on 'em would take twenty to make a paound, and some wouldn't take mor'n eight, an' where'd yer cookin' go ter, I'd like ter know?

MRS. G. Waal, Nathan, I don't care nuthin' abaout that! I shall put twelve eggs inter my old-fashioned paound cake, as the recipee sez, whether they're big or little. But I do care about the caarf. I'd almost ruther you'd 'a' sold *me!*

CAPT. G. Wall, I vum to vummy!

MRS. G. You knew haow much I allus tho't on her 'cause little Sally loved her so; an' 'a'ore she died she'd be'n a-readin' some o' them old pictur'-books, an' she said the caarf had eyes

just like one on 'em in it, an' so she named the caarf May
Donna, or some sich name. (*Wipes her eyes.*)

CAPT. G. Consarn it all! Lorany, don't cry! There!
There! I'll pick up the money, Lorany, I'll pick up the
money. (*Aside*) I wonder if there *is* anything in them wimmin's rights, after all! (*Puts the money in his pocket. Sits
in chair tipped back against the wall, and eats an apple, cut-
ting it with his jack-knife.*)

(*Enter* LEAFY JANE *and* JOHN QUINCY ADAMS, *the latter
dragging a small log of wood.*)

MRS. G. (*looking up*). Where yer be'n all the arternoon?

J. Q. A. Ben to the wharf, chippin'.

L. J. (*lisping*). Yeth, we chipped and got our bathketh
full, and the thkipperth (*skipper's*) boy, he thed, 'There, take a
log'—and we took one.

CAPT. G. The skipper's boy!—who's he?

J. Q. A. He's the skipper's son.

CAPT. G. What skipper's son?

J. Q. A. Why! the captain of the Betsey Ludgitt. He's
down there to the wharf, unloadin' his wood. And his boy,
he's real hunkey! He give me all these butnuts (*shows them*)
and this gum,—see this gum,—real spruce gum!—none
o' your Burgundy pitch and candle-grease, such as you buy
to the store.

MRS. G. Gum! Then I s'pose you'll go to chawin' agin!

J Q. A. I ll bet I will. It's rippin' good! (*Chews.*)

L. J (*lisps*). Marm, he sthiks hith cud on the head-board,
and it makth a white plathe. I theen it when I make the
bed.

MRS. G. Sticks his cud on the head-board! What on
airth do you mean?

L. J. Yeth, hith cud o' gum. He doth it motht every
night, when he *hath* gum.

MRS. G. What do you do that for?

J. Q. A. I stick it there when I go to sleep, so when I
wake up in the middle of the night I can have a good chaw
to pass away the time.

CAPT. G. Haw! Haw! Haw!

MRS. G. John Quincy Adams Gandy! What 'll yer do next!

J. Q. A. Go a-fishin', I guess, marmy. (*Kisses her.*)

CAPT. G. What's the skipper's name?

J. Q. A. Miller — Solomon Miller; and his son's name's William.

L. J. And the cook'th name ith Henry Mudgett.

MRS. G. The cook! What der yer know abaout the cook?

L. J. He'th real nithe. I thaw him lath fall. Hith mother an' grandfather live down to Nantucket. Hith grand-father thalth (*salts*) down fith, nam'th (*name's*) Zabulon, and they have a big houth an' a lot of land.

CAPT. G. A lot o' sand, I guess you mean. Haow'd yer come ter know 'em so well!

J. Q. A. Oh! They was up here in the fall when we went a-chippin' with Mary, and they talked with us a good deal.

L. J. Yeth, an' the thkipper'th thon kept lookin' at Mary.

J. Q. A. Yes, and so did Hank at you.

L. J. Hith name ain't Hank! it'h Henry!

J. Q. A. Oh, Lawks!

MRS. G. Whar *is* Mary?

J. Q. A. We left her down to the wharf, an' she was a talkin' to the skipper's son.

L. J. Yeth, and the thkipper came out, and he talked, an' they all laughed, and he thed to John Pin, "Run along, Totty, with your log o' wood. They'll foller ye, an' tell yer pa an' ma all about it."

J. Q. A. I guess I aint Totty! (*Chewing.*) I seen 'em an' after they done it, —

L. J. Oh, John Pin Ad! you muthn't thay 'I theen,' *Mary* theth. You can't thay 'theen' nor 'done,' unleth you can thay have' before it; an' you can't thay 'I theed,' at all.

J. Q. A. I guess I can too. Mary needn't feel so big 'cause she's ben to Bradford 'cademy three months.

L J Yeth, you mutht thay 'I have thawed,' and 'I hain't theen,' and 'I have did,' and 'I hain't done it,' and you'll be right.

J. Q A. Poh! you ain't right at all! Hear me. You must say 'I have done, I have seen,' or 'I saw and I did '; and you must never say ' I seed, I sawed, I seen,' nor ' I done it.' That's what *Mary* says.

L J. Father thayth 'I theen and I done'; and I gueth what father theth ith about right.

CAPT. G. O child! Yer mustn't talk as I do. Mary knows what's proper to say, better'n yer old dad. He never had no edication. There was no 'cademy for him.

MRS G. Nor me, nuther. Gals wa'n't 'lowed to go to school in my time, daown to Plymouth, when my folks lived there. There was too many boys wanted to go ; and the gals had to stay ter hum, to make room for 'em.

(*Enter* MARY *and* WILLIAM.)

MARY. Father, here's Captain Miller's son. I made his acquaintance down at the wharf last fall. (*Goes to* MRS. G., *seats herself on a stool near her, and arranges rags, and hands them to her.*)

CAPT. G. (*rising and shaking hands with* WILL). Is that so ?

WILL. Yes! and, when I went home, I told the folks all about her and the children, and the Captain and Mrs. Gandy ; and mother said one of her girl friends, a real intimate, married a Gandy.

MRS. G. What was her name afore she was married?

WILL. Johnson.

MRS. G. Plumy Johnson, as I'm alive!

WILL. Yes, her name was Plumy — Plumy Johnson.

MRS. G. (*shaking his hand*) Wal, if I ain't right glad ter see yer. Set right daown an' tell us all abaout your folks.

WILL (*sitting*). There ain't much to tell. Father, he's skipper of the Betsey Ludgitt, and we live in North Pittston, Maine. We've got a nice little place there, and there's ten of us children. I am the oldest.

CAPT. G. (*sitting*). Haow long yer be'n skippin'?

WILL. About five years. I've got so now I can handle a boat, and one of the other boys is going to take my place.

CAPT. G. What are you goin' ter dew?

WILL. There's a man out West, clear beyond the Ohio, that wants me to run a boat on the Mississippi, up and down. It's a steamboat. He's got a good mate for her that knows all about the ingine, and he says I can learn the ropes about that fast enough. But I don't know. I hate to go so far from home, and almost alone too. (*He looks conscious.*)

MRS. G. I should think yer would. Don't stand gawpin' raound, Leafy Jane. Go 'long and git yer knittin'-work. (L. J. *obeys and seats herself on the log.* J. Q. A. *bothers her.*) And yer marm, what does she say?

WILL. Oh! marm, she hates to have me go; but she's more willing than she would be, 'cause Hank Mudgitt, a likely Nantucket boy, wants to go with me, to be the cook. He's been cooking for father. His marm was a Folger, and knew my marm when she lived to Nantucket, and she says I'd better not lose the chance.

CAPT. G. Folger? Folger? Why! I've heerd that name afore. I knew a Captain Folger onct, of the barque Hulda Griggs. He had a lot o' boys, an' one on 'em went to college, and turned out a smart lawyer. I guess yer'd better not lose the chance. Lots o' boys go West, and they do well, or they don't come back to tell us. Horace Greeley told 'em all to go West, in his *Trybune*, you know, when he wrote the whole on't. "Go West, young man," he says, though he didn't go himself. But I s'pose his advice was jest as good, same as the guide-board p'ints the way it never goes.

WILL. The man that wants me says it's a good steamboat, with a nice, clean cabin for a family to live in, if a captain had one.

CAPT. G. Is it a side-wheeler or a skre-you?

J. Q. A. Oh! father, all them Mississippi steamboats are side-wheelers, and they have to be made flat-bottomed on account of the snags in the river, and the shallow water, so's they can run 'em right up to the shore, where there 's no landing. Oliver Optic says so in one of his books.

CAPT. G.   Dew tell! I'd ruther have a sailin' vessel.   Give me a good three-masted schaouner, with a spankin' breeze to make her go, and a bower anchor to cast when she comes inter port.

WILL.   The man says he'll pay me so much a year, enough to live on, and give me a certain per cent on the freight, and a chance to buy into the vessel in two years.

CAPT. G.   A smackin' good chance, I should say.   I advise yer to snap at it.   When does he want ye ?

WILL.   Right off, in a month or so, and now, if I could get anybody, besides Hank Mudgitt, to go with me (*looks at* MARY), I shall write right off and accept the offer.

CAPT. G.   Somebody ter go with ye besides Hank! What do you want anybody else for? Ain't he a good cook ?

MRS. G.   What on airth do you mean ?

WILL. (*to* CAPT. G.)   Yes, but I want somebody, some-body to be — my — wife.

CAPT. G.   Dew tell !   What kind of a wife do yer want ? Not one o' them gals that wears bangs an' boot-heels, an' go a-teetering along the road ?

WILL.   No, I don't want one of that kind.   Mary — Mary says she'll go with me if you are both willing.

MRS. G.   Aour Mary !   Mary Gandy !

CAPT. G.   Wal, I swan to man !

MRS. G.   Why !   Mary, where'd he git a chance to ask yer?

MARY.   I saw him first, mother, as I told you, last fall, when I went down to the wharf with the children, chipping. You know you didn't want them to go alone.   He said then he should come back in the spring, and hoped he'd see me again.

WILL.   And I have seen her several times ; and the other day I told her about the steamboat, and she 'lowed she was willing to go with me.

MRS. G. I thought she was 'mazin' fond o' chippin' all to onct.

MARY. I guess you mean that 'I promised,' don't you, William?

WILL. Yes, you promised, and I told father; and he said he guessed it was all right. He'd known o' Captain Gandy quite a spell. The Nancy Paige lay at the wharf alongside the Betsey Ludgitt once, down to Castine.

J. Q. A. (*trying to mend a whip-lash*). By darn!

L. J. My Thunday-thkool teacher theth you muthn't thay *by darn*; but if you mutht thay *by anything*, you can thay *by jollerth* (*jollers*).

J. Q. A. I saw the skipper's son kiss Mary, and she kissed him just as he give me a log o' wood. (*Singing derisively.*) Kissin' the fellers, kissin' the fellers!

(WILL *rises in confusion, and goes to back of stage.*)

MRS. G. Stop! John Quincy Adams Gandy!

CAPT. G. (*walking about*). I snum to pucker. Wal! seein' it's all made up between yer, I don't see as we have anything to do abaout it.

MRS. G. I don't know as it would do any good for me to say no, even if I wanted to. (*To* WILLIAM) Haow long you goin' to be raound here?

WILL. Another week. Then I must go home with father to get my things and what money I've saved up, then come back and buy the fixings to furnish the cabin with. If Mary's ready by that time, we will start for the Mississippi about the first of June.

CAPT. G. Better come here every day, and let us see something of ye. P'r'aps Mary will conclude not to go, if she sees too much on ye.

MRS. G. Yes. Come right here and stay. I feel as if Plumy Johnson's son must be a good boy; an', if Mary is set on havin' ye, I want to get some acquainted with my new son-in-law. (MARY *rises and crosses to* WILLIAM.)

L. J. I geth he ain't the only thon-in-law you'll have, mother.

MRS. G. I hope he'll be so good that I shall want another.

J. Q. A. (*trying to snap* L. J.'s *ears*). I s'pose you want to be a loveress, too. (*Makes up a face.*)

L. J.   *You* won't be.

J. Q. A.   I will, too.

L. J.   You won't, nuther. (*Makes up a face.*)

> Old Phin Gan-dowdy,
> He'th an' old rowdy.

J. Q. A.   This is the way you'll look when you are a loveress. (*Imitates a fine young lady.*) How are you, Hank! Mrs. Henry Mudgitt!

L. J.   Go way — you gump!

MRS. G.   Do, children, stop yer bickerin'! (*To* MARY) I declare for't' I hate to hev yer go so far from hum. But, then (*with a sigh*), my mother lives e'en a'most to the jumpin'-off place daown East; and I hain't seen her this five year.

CAPT. G. (*goes to* MRS. G. *and puts hand on her shoulder*). It's the way o' natur', mother. The Bible says: "A man shall leave his father and mother, an' shall be united to his wife."

J. Q. A.   Well, father, it don't say *she* shall. It says *he*.

CAPT. G.   It means the same, any way. The Bible allus means she when it says he. It means 'em both. Genesis says, yer know, chap. V., verse 2, Male and female created he them, an' blessed them, an' called their name Adam, in the day when they was created. The Bible said that in the beginning. Even old Pete Rosson allows that.

MRS. G.   I wonder yer hadn't thought o' that when yer sold my caarf, *aour* caarf, mine as well as yourn.

CAPT. G. (*walking off*). I van! I never did.

MRS. G.   If he did creat' men an' wimmin ekal, an' call their name Adam, just as we call aourn Gandy, one on us has no right to sell the things that belong to both without askin' each other's leave.

CAPT. G. (*returning*). I don't s'pose they have, Lorany. If yer don't beat 'em all in an argiment. (*Aside*) Hang that caarf! Come, mother, don't let's bicker any more abaout that. (*To* MARY) Yer'll have quite a weddin' tower, won't ye, Mary, 'way out on to the Mississippi? Yer'll have ter work spry ter git yer weddin' toggery ready. Whar yer goin' ter be married ; ter hum ?

MRS. G. Lucky I saved my old receipee for weddin' cake.

WILL. We think we'd better go to the minister's, and have it done quiet like, the very morning before we start. We sha'n't feel like making much of a touse about it, 'cause everybody 'll be crying to see Mary go off.

MRS. G. And, then, our relations live so far off, they couldn't any on' em come. Lucky yer made them sheets, Mary. Yer wouldn't 'a' had half time enough naow to get 'em done.

CAPT. G. I van! mother. It reminds me o' the time when we went to live on the Nancy Paige.

MRS. G. So it does me.

CAPT. G. There's nothing like the sea to live on, is there, mother ? (*Sings.*)

> " I'm on the sea,
> I am where I would ever be,
> The deep, the dark, the rolling sea."

MARY. You'll have to sing it " river " for us, father.

J. Q. A. (*takes up the refrain, and snaps his whip at the end of each line*).

> I am where I would ever be-iver,
> The deep, the dark, the rolling re-iver.

L. J. Thtop! you thap-head (*sap-head*), you thilly coot ! (WILLIAM *and* MARY *whisper together.*)

CAPT. G. I guess I'll go an' fodder them caows. (*Humming.*)

> " An' turnin' raound he straight did feel
> A pywison sarpient byite hywis hee-ee-el."

(*Exit* R.)

WILL. (*taking* MARY *by both hands*). Be all ready, now Mary, when I come back? If I can, I'll come on so as to stay a day or two before we're married. But I'll be here in season, any way. You fix the day, and let me know. And write often (*whispers*), dear Mary, won't you?

MARY. Yes, William.

WILL. Good-by!

MARY. Good-by! (*Exit* WILLIAM, L.)

J. Q. A. Good-by! Good-by! Smack, smack!

Disposition of characters at end of Act I. MRS. G. *sitting at table braiding mat.* MARY *standing at left, with her hands clasped before her, looking down.* J. Q. A. *and* L. J. *in centre, bickering.*

ACT II.

Cabin of the Creole Bride, a Mississippi steamboat cosily furnished. Doors R. *and* L. *Table and cradle* C. *Pictures. Four books on a little shelf. A parasol and handkerchief lie on the table.* MARY, *the* CAPTAIN'S *wife, sits by the cradle sewing.*

MARY (*sings*).

"By low baby,
By low baby,
By low baby,
By low by."

(*Rises.*)

There! he's asleep at last. He keeps awake just as long as he can, I do believe. (*Takes a book from the shelf.*) I don't know what I should do this stormy weather, I am sure, if it weren't for these books. Away up here, on this river, where we don't get a newspaper but once in two weeks!

(*Turns over the books.*) I am tired of "Baxter's Saint's Rest," and I know "Alonzo and Melissa" by heart. I suppose I ought to read my Bible more, but here's this book on navigation. (*Reads.*) "Thoms' Navigator," by Janet Thorms, a Yankee schoolmarm, they say, up near Boston. It seems fresh all the time. I like to study it, too, when I am rocking the cradle. (*Sits and reads.*) Somehow, it seems to come natural to me to know all about a boat, and I love any kind of a one. How they skip round the bend of the river, and over the sea, at home! I wonder why they call a vessel *she!* Father says they ought to call steamboats *he*, because they smoke so. Dear father! how I should like to see him, and hear him sing!

(*Enter* PHUS, R.)

PHUS (*in a loud voice*). Mis', de cap'n say —

MARY. Sh ! you'll wake the baby.

PHUS (*in a loud whisper*). Mis', de cap'n dun tole me he not feel well, an' you come to de weel-house. Phus tote de baby.

MARY (*rising hastily*). Take good care of him. (*Exit* R.)

PHUS. Take good care ob *him*. (*Imitates her voice, and tip-toes round the room.*) How golly fine it am to be de cap'n's mis', a-sittin' down har all fix' up, and den walkin' on deck wid de par-sol, totin' de baby. Oh, Lor! (*Sings softly.*)

> Min' de pick'niny,
> Min' de pick'niny,
> Take good care ob *him*.

Wot's dem books ? I dunno, caze I can't read 'em all yit. But the cap'n's mis', she try larn me. Lemme see. (*Takes up a book and reads.*) "Meel-iss-see-felt-a-cold-han'-on-her-fore- head - an' - she - scream - ded - scream - ded." Wot's dat ? Golly! I can't do dat. (*Shuts up the book.*) Sh! sh ! de baby's wokem up. He'll holler ef he see me.

I'll make him tink I'm de cap'n's mis'. (*He takes the parasol and opens it, spreads the handkerchief over his face, and sits down by the cradle. Enter* CAPTAIN MILLER, R, *leaning on* MARY'S *shoulder.*)

MARY.   Tell me, dear, just how you feel. (*Sees* PHUS.) Oh, Phus! you'll scare the baby.

PHUS.   Mis', de baby was a gwine to wokem up, and I specks he'd tink 'twas you.

CAPT. M.   Phus, take off that rig, and go on deck, you lubber! (*Exit* PHUS, R.) Oh, I don't know.   I feel just as I did once when I was a boy, before I had the typhoid fever, — tired all over. (*Sits.*)   My head is as light as a feather, and my feet are heavy as lead.   I don't feel as if I could step a step.

MARY.   Lie down a little while, and perhaps you'll feel better.   How much farther do we go up river?

CAPT. M.   About two hundred miles.   We shall reach the last station in a few days. (*Takes off his jacket and shoes wearily, as he talks.*)   Patsy is at the wheel, and you can bring me word if he wants anything.

MARY (*aside*).   Oh, dear! I know he is going to be sick. (*To him*)   Where is the chart of the river?

CAPT. M.   On deck, in the wheel-house.

MARY.   And all the things you use?

CAPT. M.   Yes.   Why?

MARY.   Because I want to know, so that you can have a good long nap.

CAPT. M.   Our course is all marked out, and what to steer by; but I shall feel better, I hope, after I have had some sleep.   You'd better go on deck, once in a while, see how things are going on, and let me know. (*Exit* L., *holding by the doorway.*)

MARY (*sitting*).   What shall I do! away up here, a hundred miles from a doctor.   I am afraid William has the river fever, the same as Phus had last year.   Oh! mother! mother!   If I could only have you with me!   If I could only get word to you! (*Leans her head on the table.*)

(*Enter* PHUS, R.)

PHUS. Whar de cap'n? Pats say he want know which way ter go, and de cap'n must tell him.

MARY. Phus, do you remember how sick you were last year?

PHUS. An' I wouldn't 'a' libed ef you hadn't 'a' nussed me.

MARY. Do you want to pay me for it?

PHUS. I ain't got no money, mis'; but I prays ebery night: Lor' bress de cap'n's wife. She nuss me; make me well.

MARY. I don't want any money, Phus. You can pay me in a better way.

PHUS. An' I sings in de cook-house w'en de pork's a-fizzlin', an' Hank he likes it. (*Sings mournfully.*)

> I'se poor Jo-Phus, — 'Lijah cum down.
> Sick in de 'teamboat, — 'Lijah cum down.
> Cap'n's mis' nuss me, — 'Lijah cum down.
> (*Livelier.*) An' den I gits well, — 'Lijah cum down.
> Swing low de goolden charyot,
> Rock de baby, car' long de cap'n's mis'.
> 'Lijah cum down.

(MARY *does not listen.*)

MARY. Phus, listen to me. The captain is very sick, and you can help me if you will; and more than pay me for anything I have done for you.

PHUS. I'll do ebryting. You so good to poor Phus — make me well, an' larn me to read — see here. (*Reads.*) "Mee-liss-see-felt-a-scream-ded," no, dat ain't de place; "col' — col' — han' — " (*cold hand.*)

MARY. Never mind reading now, Phus. I want you to stay here while I go on deck, and listen to the captain. If he wakes up and wants anything, you must go in and tell him I will come right down; then you come and call me. (*Exit* R.)

PHUS. Yaas, mis'! (*Applies ear to keyhole of door*, L.)

CURTAIN.

ACT III.

Forward deck of the Creole Bride. Wheel-house at R. *gangway and railing at* L., *table and two camp chairs at* C., *chairs* C. MARY *at the wheel, with the chart and compass beside her.*

MARY. I wonder if I am all right here! The course is not very clearly marked out. Willie is still so sick that he can't tell me any more about steering, and Patsy don't seem to know anything but his engine, or how to go when it is plain sailing. (*Studies the chart.*) Let me see! We must stop at three more stations before we reach the mouth of the Washita, — Munroe, Columbia, and Harrisonburg ; and then we go down the Red and Yellow to Baton Rouge. Oh! yes, I see. We steer right here by Dead Man's Bluff, and then by Run-away Swamp. How lucky I studied that book on navigation! It helps me so much to understand these marks on the chart. If Patsy would only behave well, I should be all right; but he don't like the idea of being "bossed," as he calls it, "by a woman."

(*Enter* PATSY, R.)

MARY. Patsy, have you thrown out the line lately?

PATSY. Yes, mum.

MARY. Where are we?

PATSY. Be-gorries! I dunno, mum.

MARY. How much water?

PATSY. Faix! the lid was varry well down, and the mud was yaller.

MARY. That may mean something to you, I suppose. You can't read. Bring me the line. (*He bring it from* L.)

PATSY. It's tin fut, mum. (*Aside*) Bedad, she thinks she's cap'n.

MARY. That'll do. Take the line forward, and mind your engine.

PATSY (*muttering*). Mind the injun, is it? O' coorse. Musha and faix, I wull! I'm the lasht lad not to be mindin' me injun. (*Drops the line and goes toward* R.)

MARY. Patsy!

PATSY. Vart do yer want? I can't be lavin' my injun arl the time. True for yez!

MARY. Patsy! I told you to take the line *forward!*

PATSY. I'll not do it, mum, for all of yez. Ye're not the cap'n!

MARY (*looking at him severely*). Patsy! Take that line *forrard*, and be quick about it!

PATSY (*takes the line to* L., *and exit* R., *muttering*). I'll not be bossed by no woman!

MARY. I don't know what I shall do with Patsy. He threatens to leave me at the next station, and I can't find a decent engineer short of Baton Rouge; and I mustn't trouble William with it, he is still so feeble.

(*Enter* PHUS, L.)

PHUS. Mis', de cap'n say he feel bet' as did, an' he wan' ter see yer.

MARY. Very well, I'll go down. You call Patsy to stand at the wheel; and then you go and stay with the baby.

PHUS. Yes, mis'. (*Calls,* R.) Pats! Har! you Pats, lave dat injyne an' cum an' stan' by de wheel. Pay—ats! Pay—ats! Pay—a—ts! Cum, Pats, to de weel-house! Mis' say so.

(*Enter* PATS R. *He takes the wheel.*)

MARY (*to* PATSY). Mind your helm now; keep her on her course. (*Exit* MARY, R.)

PATSY. Ugh! Bedad!

PHUS (*sits down at the wheel-house and takes his banjo*). Bress de Lor', de cap'n's bet' as was. He say he mean git well. (*Sings and rocks himself.*)

Lor' bress de cap'n, — 'Lijah **cum down.**
Lor' bress de cap'n's mis', — 'Lijah cum **down.**
An' let 'im git well, — 'Lijah cum down.
As dis poor Jo-Phus **did,** — 'Lijah cum down.
Swing low de goolden charyot,
Car' long de baby, cap'n, an' de cap'n's mis',
            'Lijah cum down.

PATSY (*putting his head out of the wheel-house*). Musha!
Shtop yer hullabaloo, **you** black nayger.

PHUS. Dere ain't no sich man **round here.** My name's
Jo-see-phus, Herodytus Miller. (**Exit L.**)

(*Re-enter* MARY, R., *half supporting* CAPTAIN MILLER,
who tries to walk; he sits down near the table wearily.)

CAPT. M. (*feebly*). It's no use, Mary, I can't walk. I
can't use my legs a mite, and that's a fact. The malaria has
settled in them, and I don't know **as I shall ever** walk
again.

MARY (*stands beside him, and keeps her eye on the vessel's
course*). Yes, you will, dear. The doctor says so; and he
says you must get away from the boat, go into the mountains **and** stay **awhile,** and then you will be as well **as**
ever.

CAPT. M. Oh, Mary! **If I** could only go to **New** England.
I feel as if it would cure me. If I could only go to Maine,
and see the White Hills, all covered with snow on top, from
behind father's **house,** see mother, and have some of their
good victuals — (*He breaks down.*)

MARY. You *shall* go. It won't **cost any more to** go
there than it will to pay your board **at some place** near the
mountains; and no matter if it does.

CAPT. M. How can I leave the vessel? If I take the
money to go East with, I sha'n't be able to meet my payments, and shall lose my **chance** of buying into her.

MARY (*to* PATSY). **Ease her off a couple** of points. (*To*
WILLIAM) Never **mind** that! **Don't worry.** It's better to
lose everything else than to lose your health. But you will
not lose the boat. **I can run her** while you're **gone.** Only

three months! The doctor says he thinks that will do.

CAPT. M. I don't know about your running the boat, Mary. Ours is a thousand-mile trip, you know, next time, and it's easier to come down than it is to go up. The Yellow-red winds like a corkscrew.

MARY. I know that, William; but I think I can manage her. I have done it; and here we are safe so far, and no accident yet.

CAPT. M. (*considering*). This cargo is secure. and the next one all promised. But I hate to leave you, Mary, and the baby.

MARY (*to* PATSY). Keep her on her course, boy! (*To* WILLIAM) I hate to have you go, William, only I know that it is for your good; and then, if I go. you'll have to give up the boat, and we sha'n't have anything to live on; and that will never do.

CAPT. M. You're right, Mary, as you always are.

(*Enter* HANK, *the cook, with a waiter full of dishes.*)

HANK. Here's your lunch, sir.

CAPT. M. Why, Hank! Have *you* come again? It isn't more than half an hour since I ate my breakfast.

HANK (*drawling*). Yes, it is, sir. It's an hour. And the doctor says you was to eat every hour.

CAPT. M. (*looks at the waiter*). What have you got now?

MARY (*to* PATSY, *hurriedly*). Hard a-port, there! Give that snag a wide berth! (*She goes quickly towards the wheel-house.*) Go below, Patsy, and fire up, or we sha'n't get to Munroe till moonrise. (*Exit* PATSY, L., *muttering.*)

HANK (*to* WILLIAM). Waal, tha's some fixings the Indians say is good for invaliges, and one on 'em showed me how to cook 'em.

CAPT. M. What are they. Hank? Name over your bill of fare.

HANK. Waal, cap, this ere's corn-pone. o' coose; and a dodger or so; a slice o' bacon; a helter-skelter; some succotash ; two frog's legs pealed and sizzled ; a pigeon biled in milk ; some baked punkin ; eel's tails soused ; and some no-cake.

CAPT. M.   What! what! what!   Are you going to stuff me to death, or poison me — which?

HANK.   Oh, sir! you needn't eat 'em all.   The Injuns said if you eat just the right thing for you, you'd be sure to get well.

CAPT. M.   I dare say.   They'd cure a dog with their charms and their notions.

HANK.   Some of the vittals is good, and some pretty mid-dlin' poor, but it's all good for suthin', — or the pigs !

CAPT. M. (*laughing*).   I shouldn't wonder. (*Looking over the waiter.*)   What's baked punkin for, Hank ?   It looks like raw, dried potato-parings.

HANK.   The Indians said 'twas to chaw, and give you an appetite.

MARY (*from the wheel-house*).   What in the world are the soused eel's-tails for ?

HANK.   Oh, to make you feel lively, and cherk you up a little.   They make brains.

CAPT. M.   What next ?   What's the no-cake for, and where is it ?   Cake sounds kind o' good.   And hot biscuit.   Mother's hot biscuit!   Oh! how I should like some of them.

HANK.   Well, the no-cake is that aire white stuff piled up on that aire plate.   It looks like something goodish; but when you chaw it, it feels like sand.   The Injuns eat it, and they said 'twould make the cap'n sleep good.

CAPT. M.   I should think it would, — and dream of my grandmother.   If it chews like sand, it will be heavy enough.

HANK.   There ain't no decent vittals for a sick man to eat in these diggings.   'Tain't half so good as the Nantucket feed, such as my marm used to cook.

CAPT. M.   Oh, Hank! don't speak of it!   How I should like some fried perch, — some good fresh salt-water perch,

with their heads on ; and some steamed clams, fresh-dug
Nantucket clams, with the shells all gaping at you. I feel as
if I could eat a good four-quart tin pan full this minute,
shells and all.

HANK. I'd like to make you a rippin' good chowder, sir.
Such as we have ter hum. What you want is real, good,
hard, fresh cod-fish or haddock, head and all, some white
potatoes (none o' your flat yellow sweets), some onions, some
Boston crackers, and a generous rasher of salt strip pork
(none o' your middlings). But I can't do it. They never
heerd of a Boston cracker, and there ain't a decent piece o'
fresh salt-water fish between here and Nantucket. Only
this darned canned stuff; and that's enough to p'isen a
feller. •

MARY (*to* WILLIAM, *from the wheel-house*). You'll have
some chowder when you get home, dear ; and you'll eat
again of all the old New England food.

HANK. Oh, sir! you goin' hum ?

CAPT. M. I think of it.

MARY (*to* HANK). Yes, he *is* going home ; and pretty
soon, too.

HANK. If you do, sir, I hope you'll take a skip down to
Nantucket, and see my folks. Marm 'll be mighty glad to
see you. I'll write to her, and send her some money, and
you can take the letter, sir, right along. And please, sir,
fetch me word how the old place looks, and if marm seems
comfortable.

CAPT. M. Yes, Hank, I'll take your letter ; and if I can't
go to see your mother, I will send it to her by express.

HANK. Thank you, sir, thank you ; and if you should go
to Annisport, and see Miss Leafy Jane, please tell her I
hain't forgot her, and if you can say I've been a good feller —
and behaved tip-top —

CAPT. M. Why, Hank ! do you remember that little fly-
away ? You steady old boy, you. Of course you've been a
good fellow, and I'll tell her so, — if I see her, — but why
don't you write to her yourself?

HANK.   Oh, sir ! she might not like it.

CAPT. M.   That's so.   Well, do as you like, Hank.
You can leave the waiter.   I will eat all I can of your con-
coctions.   (*Exit* HANK, R.)

CAPT. M. (*turning towards* MARY).   I did not know that
there was any love-making in that quarter.

MARY.   Nor I, neither.

[*Disposition of characters at end of act.* CAPT. MILLER
at table, C., *eating.* MARY *at the wheel*, L.]

CURTAIN.

———

ACT IV.

The same as in Act II.   Enter MARY, L., *with her hands
full of papers.   She sits down at the table.*

MARY.   There!   The bills of lading are signed, and all
my accounts are straight, so we are ready to begin again.
But here we are, still fast at New Orleans, when we
ought to have got away three days ago.   For some reason or
other I can't get the cargo that was promised, and so I have
had to fill up with watermelons.   Heavy, unprofitable things !
(*Writes.*)   I wish I could hear from William.   Poor fellow !
The doctor at home said he must take a sea-voyage ; and he
has gone off with his father to the Grand Banks, fishing.   I
wish I could see him !

(*Enter* PHUS, R., *bringing a large watermelon.*)

PHUS.   Wattermillions is bos' ; dey's bos' an' cool.

MARY.   Why, Phus, what do you want of that watermelon ?

PHUS.   It's such a golly big one ; and den it's marked so
peart.

MARY. Why! there's hundreds of them on board just as good.

PHUS. O no! mis', dere ain't. Dis one hab de little Voudoo mark dat show dey's sweet; an' I wanted de baby to stick his little toof in it, an' suck de juice. Oh, Lors! (*Smacks his lips and sings.*)

" Some are pa'shel to de appel, oddahs clamor fo' de plum ;
Some fin' 'joyment in de cherry, oddahs make de peaches hum ;
Some git fas'ned to de onion, oddahs lub de arti-choke ;
But my taste an' wattahmillion er' bound by a pleasant joke.

" Hit er meller, hit er juicy,
Hit er coolin', hit er sweet !
Hit er painless ter de stummick —
Yo' kin eat, an' eat, an' eat ! "

I helped you bring 'em on board, didn't I, mis' ?

MARY. Yes, Phus ; you're always handy. I wish you could be the mate, in Patsy's place, and help me steer the boat.

PHUS. Lor' bress you, mis' ! I couldn't do dat. I should steer for all de snags in de riber ; an' git twisted all up in de bay-yous, an' run inter all de san'bars.

MARY. Have you found anybody yet to take Patsy's place, if he leaves ?

PHUS. No, mis'. All de boys dey say as dey won't be de mate to no woman. Dey say you has no licens', an' can't be de cap'n. An' Mass' Rumberg, he cum an' take away de Keyhole's Bride.

MARY. Oh, Phus ! is that what they say ? Then that is the reason that I could not get the cargo that was promised here ; and when they knew, too, that I had been running the boat these three months all alone !

PHUS. When de cap'n cum hum ?

MARY. Not until December, Phus.

PHUS. Whar's he, mis', now ?

MARY. Away out to sea, on a ship ; not a steamboat —

a sailing vessel. The doctor said it would cure him if he took a sea-voyage.

PHUS.   Is de sea bigger dan de Missip' or de Gulf Mex'?

MARY.   Oh, yes, Phus! a good deal bigger, and wider, too.   You can't see across.

PHUS.   O, sho!

MARY (*rising and walking about*).   And the waves are so high! and white on the top! and they come booming in on the rocks! and the breeze!   Oh! the breeze is so sweet, so salt, so fresh!   It is enough to do your soul good to smell it.

PHUS.   Golly! mis'.   It mus' be hunky, if it's sweet, and salt, and fresh, an' comes in boomin' at ye, on de rocks, all at once.

MARY (*smiling*).   Better go out again, Phus, and look among the boys for a mate.

PHUS.   Yes, mis'.   (*Exit* R.)

MARY.   I think I'll write to mother, and tell her my troubles.   If she can't help me any, it will do me good to write; and I can get Phus to carry it to the Post Office before we start.   (*She writes.*)

(*Enter* MR. ROMBERG.)

MR. R. (*slowly and deliberately*).   Mrs. Miller, I came to see what you were going to do about the boat.   Your husband has been gone a long time; and it seems there is no prospect of his immediate return.   So we might as well talk the matter over now as at any other time.

MARY (*rises and offers him a seat*).   Mr. Romberg? I don't know as I have seen you before.   You are the largest owner in the Creole Bride, I believe?   Why do you wish to know what I am going to do?   (*Sitting.*)

MR. R. (*sitting*).   I (and the other owners) don't want the boat to be eating her head off here at the wharf.

MARY.   We shall not stay here longer than this afternoon. As soon as I come to terms with my mate, I shall be ready to steam her up.

MR. R. I don't see how you can run this boat.

MARY (*rising*) Why not, sir? I *have* run her for the last three or four months. I carried her 'way up the Red and Yellow, and down again to Baton Rouge, through the most crooked part of our whole thousand-mile route; and I steered most of the time myself. The mate don't know much about handling the wheel.

MR. R. The merchants, I find, are not willing to trust you with a cargo; so I don't see but you will have to give it up. You won't be able to meet your payments; and I must look out for my own property, as well as that of the rest of the owners, for it is all in my care.

MARY. Is not Mr. Miller's contract as captain of the boat all right? It does not expire till next year. He is all paid up to the first of the month; and I hope to be able to pay the next quarter, — that is, if I can go on running the boat.

MR. R. Yes, madam; but you must understand that the contract is with *Captain Miller*, and not with his wife; that is where the trouble is. Husband and wife are not one in this business. Captain Miller's contract *is* all right, and he *is* paid up; but if he dies, the whole thing will have to be settled.

MARY (*alarmed*). But my husband is *not* dead. He is not going to die! Why can't I run the boat up to Cairo? I have a full cargo, and another is promised there. I know the route for the next three months. I have been over it all.

MR. R. (*rising*). Mrs. Miller, you cannot be a captain in name.

MARY. But, Mr. Romberg, I *am* the captain.

MR. R. No, Mrs. Miller. You may run the boat, but you cannot act as captain, — you have no license. The fact is, the law does not allow it. That is what the owners say; and we consulted a lawyer, and he gave it as his opinion, *after careful consideration*, that a woman cannot be master of a vessel legally.

MARY. Then we must lose our chance of owning the boat; and I cannot raise the money needed for the support of my poor sick husband and my little baby, — just because I am a woman! Oh! Mr. Romberg! this is hard indeed!

MR. R. I suppose it is rather hard; but that is the way of the law, in Louisiana, at least, and I think all over the United States. When our fathers framed the constitution, they thought it was better that woman should be confined to the domestic sphere. The home, the home is their place, — not the decks of vessels. They wanted to protect women in their proper sphere.

MARY. Protect them! Hinder them, I should think!

MR. R. (*approaching* MARY). If Captain Miller, now, were not living, you might find some likely river-man to marry you, and be captain of the boat, in name; and then you could keep on acting as master, — your mate, perhaps, — then you'd be all right.

MARY. Marry! The mate! Patsy! Oh, Mr. Romberg! Oh, sir! what do you mean?

MR. R. (*aside*). Gad! the women are all alike. How they stick to one man! (*To her*) I don't see what else you can do.

MARY. There was Captain Tucker's wife; after he died she took the boat.

MR. R. Yes, but she did not run it long; all of us owners objected to a petticoat captain, and we discharged her.

MARY (*severely*). Then what has become of her and all her six children?

MR. R. Oh, she tends in a lager-beer saloon in Natchez.

MARY (*indignantly*). Yes, and I suppose her children are given away or put out to service — all because she is a woman! She has to do this degrading work to get an honest living, and all because you wouldn't allow her to do the only work she always had done and was best fitted to do. She run the boat three years before her husband died.

MR. R. Well, she might have married and had some one

to be her captain. The merchants sent one of their best river-men to marry her, but she ordered him off the boat.

MARY. I don't blame her!

MR. R. There ain't much a woman can do round here *but* get married. There's many a likely man that is *not* a river-man who would like to get a good smart Yankee woman like you.

MARY (*sharply*). Mr. Romberg! what do you mean?

MR. R. I mean, of course, if your husband does not come back, which seems most likely —

MARY (*turning away*). Oh! What shall I do?

MR. R. My dear Mrs. Miller! you must be as wise as a serpent as well as harmless as a dove.

MARY. Oh, sir! how can I be wise without money, without friends, with my hands tied by a little child, and my means of earning a living taken away?

MR. R. Well, there is a month or two yet before I shall be obliged to ask you to give up your husband's papers. Meanwhile, you can go on to Cairo, and come back; go along the Red and Yellow, and leave your cargo. You needn't take on any more. I'll see you again when you come down to New Orleans; and then, if your husband has not returned, we must close up our accounts. That is what the rest of the owners say, and I agree.

MARY. Oh, Mr Romberg! is there nothing I can do to keep the boat? Can I not get a license? Did a woman never have a captain's license?

MR. R. I never heard of one. And I don't think there ever was one. It would be absurd! But I must bid you good-morning.

MARY. Good-morning, sir. (*Exit* MR. ROMBERG, R.) Indeed! what kind of a woman does he take me to be! Telling *me* about marrying another man so as to have a captain! I will show him that I can be master of my own boat. *I* go into a lager-beer saloon! As Mary Gandy I would not have done it; and as Mary Miller I certainly shall not. *I* give up the boat! My William's boat? Never! Unless they put me on shore by force. *Why* cannot *I* get a license? *I'll try!* and then, if worst comes to worst, I must make my way somehow back home again. If I could only hear from mother! (*Sits down at the table — arranges papers.*)

(*Enter* PHUS, R.)

PHUS. O, Lor'! Mis' Miller! Here's suthin' I forgits. I met de pos'-man out here, an' he holl'd at me (*She does not look up.*) — "Har, you nig!" I looks round, and sez: "Whar? whar? I dun' see no nig." He laf, an' sez, "You know who dat is?" "Whar?" sez I. "On dis let'," sez he. "No," sez I; "who is it?" "It's Mrs. Mary Miller," sez he. "Lor'," sez I, "dat's my cap'n's mis'; gib it yere." "Well, fotch it, then," sez he, "an' be darn quick 'bout it." "I will," sez I. (MARY *looks up.*)

MARY. A letter? Oh, give it to me! How long have you had it?

PHUS. Jes dis minit, mis'.

MARY (*tearing the envelope*). From home, and written by dear brother John. Dear little fellow! (*Reads.*)

DEAR MARY, —

Mother wants me to write. She says: Tell Mary that I talked it all over with your father, and he asked old Pete Rosson, and then I wrote to the lecture woman up to Boston, and she says you must have a captain's license so's you can keep the boat. And she says you must apply to the Local Inspectors (here is a blank for you to fill out), and that if you pass your examination they will see that it is sent to Washington to the Solicitor of the Treasury. You must write to Mr. Le Brun or Mr. Cholmly, Local Inspectors, New Orleans, La. Do it right off before Mr. Romberg gets a chance to take away the boat. And oh! mother says you must sign your own name to the application — Mary Miller, or Mary Gandy Miller ('cause it isn't legal to sign your husband's name, and *Mrs.* is nothing but a title). She's found out that a woman has no more right, legally, to use her husband's first name and title than he has to use hers. She says Martha Washington had more sense than to call herself Mrs. George, or Mrs. General, or Mrs. President Washington. Plain

Martha Washington was good enough for her. And oh! the folks round here are real proud of you, to think you can manage a steamboat, and old Pete Rosson says "it's a darned shame you have such a hard time, and he hopes you won't give up the ship." He expects to go to the Legislature this winter, and he says "if the men at Washington don't let you have the captain's license, he'll vote agin every mother's son on 'em."

Yours, as usual,

JOHN QUINCY ADAMS GANDY.

MARY (*folding the letter*). Dear, dear folks at home! How good they are to tell me just what to do! I must write my application at once. (*Sits down at the table.*)

PHUS. Is de folks well, mis', an' de cap'n?

MARY (*writing*) Yes, Phus, the folks are well; but the letter is not from the captain. I do not expect to hear from him at present.

PHUS. O, Lor'! mis, is dat so?

MARY. Yes, Phus. You wait round till I get this letter done, then you carry it to the post-office. I want an answer from it, right off, as soon as I can get it.

PHUS. Yes, mis'. (*He goes out, L., keeps popping his head in and tiptoeing round.*)

MARY (*folding up the letter, and putting it in a long envelope*). There! my blank is all filled out, and my letter written; both signed plain Mary Miller, which means to me (*sighing*) that I must hereafter stand alone, — legally, at any rate, and take the responsibility of all my actions. No more hiding behind a husband's or a father's name. Plain Mary Miller! A good name, and I must show that I am worthy of it. (*To* PHUS) There, be as quick as you can; and then come back here and take care of the baby while I go on deck. (*She goes to the cradle.*)

PHUS. Yes, mis'! I'm skippin'. (*Exit* R.)

CURTAIN.

ACT V.

Same as in Act III., with the addition of a hammock slung near the wheel-house, containing the baby. Enter MARY *from the wheel-house with a small sailor hat and reefer on. She takes them off, and lays them on a chair as she talks.*

MARY. Here we are at last, safe at New Orleans. I wish I could hear from Washington; and why *don't* I hear from William? I sent home the last money I had saved up, and I shall have no more if they take the boat away. I can't give her up! And I can't do anything else to earn a living. This is my business — my life.

(*Enter* PHUS, L.)

PHUS. Oh, mis'! Pats he say he won't help unload de boat; an' I can't get nobody to help, as you tole me. Dey all say dey won't be bos' by no woman.

MARY (*sighs*). Well, Phus, *you're* willing to work for me, ain't you? *You* won't leave your mistress, will you?

PHUS. Neber! No, mis'! I allus work for you an' de cap'n an' de baby. Hank, too, he stay. He ben hawlin out de cargo like sixty. He say wimmin good 'nough for him. He ruther be cook to wimmin bos'; cos dey knows more 'bout de fixin's, an' dey neber sez, "darn dat stuff."

MARY. Phus, you run and tell Patsy he can go. He's all paid up; and I don't want him any more. And, here! take my reefer and hat down into the cabin. I sha'n't want them at present.

PHUS. Yes, mis'. (*He goes out,* R.)

MARY (*swinging the hammock gently*). Must I leave my happy home, where I came a bride? (*Leans over the baby*) My baby's birthplace? Why! I love every timber in this tight little steamboat. She is as dear to me as one of the biggest houses on the river is to the fine lady who lives in it.

PHUS (*re-entering*). Oh, mis'! Pats he say he *will* go wid you up riber a piece, to where he woman lib, an' get off dar.

MARY. Very well. I'll see him by and by; but I don't know as I shall want him. Oh! if my license would only come!

PHUS. You licens', mis; wot's you licens'?

MARY (*sadly*). Why, Phus, I have asked the big men at Washington to give me a license; same as the other river-captains have.

PHUS (*whimpering*). Oh, Lor', mis, bress de Lor'! I hope it'll cum. (*Sits on floor at* R., *and sings softly.*)

Bring 'long de licens',— 'Lijah cum down.

(*Takes a book from his pocket, sits on floor at* R., *and reads with a great deal of action.*)

MARY (*looking at him*). Poor Phus! If the big men at Washington could only see me as he sees me, and know, as he knows, how well I can handle a boat, they would very soon say yes to my application.

(*Enter* MR. ROMBERG, L.)

MR. R. Good-day, Mrs. Miller. I am sorry to be obliged to proceed against you, and ask you to deliver up your husband's papers. *I* might be willing to wait a little longer; but the other owners are not satisfied. They say that as you cannot get a captain's license, some man must take the boat.

MARY. Cannot get a captain's license? How do you know that? I have applied for one; and am expecting every minute to hear from Washington.

MR. R. I know that. Here is the *Delta* with a long account of your case, and the decision of the Solicitor of the Treasury.

MARY (*coming forward*). Let me see it! I have heard nothing about it. We have had no mail since we got in.

MR. R. (*reads from the newspaper emphatically*). "One of the richest papers on the woman question that has ever emanated from an official source is the opinion of Solicitor Rayner on the question whether licenses should be granted women to command steamboats. He says : 'Instead of being master in name, while some one else performs the duties, why does she not let some one else be master in name ? She would not stand her watch at night in the cold. She would not enforce the discipline on a Mississippi steamer. She would not tramp to the rooms of shippers and consigners to do the banking business — '"

MARY (*interrupting*). Why ! that is just what I have been doing for the last five months.

MR. R. (*reads on*). "'All the accounts concur in describing the lady who makes this application as one of high character, business qualifications, and highest worth. But, in the application of what is with me a principle, the higher the character and worth, the greater my difficulty in asking that the license asked for to command a Mississippi steamboat be granted. Because it would be assigning a position to woman which God, in his providence, never intended her to fill.   K. Rayner, Solicitor of the Treasury.'"

(*Holds out paper to her.*)

MARY. What does he mean ? I am sure God has permitted me to fill this position, and (*reverently*) if He had not permitted it, and helped me, too, I never could have done it so well. How unjust this man is ! Oh, Mr. Rayner ! can you not comprehend that, when a woman *can do* a man's work, she ought to have the legal right? (*Comes forward, takes the paper, and reads to herself. To him*) But see, Mr. Romberg. Here is something else about it ; something from the Secretary of the Treasury. (*Reads*) "The United States Revised Statutes say that whenever any person applies to be licensed, the inspectors shall diligently inquire as to the character of the person, whether male or female. I see no reason, then, in unwritten or in written law, why Mistress Miller may not lawfully demand an examina-

tion ; and, if she proves herself duly qualified, have a license
to serve as master of a vessel.   Let the local inspectors carefully examine her, and if they are satisfied that she can be
safely intrusted with the duties and responsibilities of a
master of a steam vessel, let them grant her a license,
according to section 4439.

       Chas. J. Folger, Secretary of the Treasury."

Bless him for that !   He may make it all right.   You see,
Mr. Romberg, it is not fully decided.   I may get the license
yet.   (PHUS *looks up from his book.*)   I have been exam-
ined ; and when I told the inspectors all about that large
boat that got stuck up the river, near Cairo, and that we had
the chance to take off the loaded barges, and how I had them
made fast to us, took the wheel myself, turned the big boat
round, and carried her safely into Cairo, they looked sur-
prised enough.   And one of them said that I did seem to be
qualified.   Phus remembers it, the visit of the inspectors ;
don't you, Phus ?

PHUS (*jumping up and putting his whole hand in the
book for a mark*).   O, yes, mis' !   dem two gem'man, one
wid de black bandanna on he hat, de oder wid de gaiters !
De las' one, he say, " You culled pusson, tel' me troo, your
mis' *she* no bos' dis boat ? "   I say, " Yaas, saar ! "   Den de
one wid de black bandanna, he say, " But de mate, *he* de real
cap'n ; *he* stan' at w'eel, steer, an' tak' car' ob injyne, don' he ? "

MARY.   What did you tell him ?

PHUS.   I sez, " No !   On'y when mis' restin', an' it's cam
(*calm*), an' dere ain't no snags nor be-yous.   *She* bos', *she*
steer, *she* watch injyne.   Pats, he on'y shovel coal, 'bey
orders.   On'y he mad sometime, an' he say he not be bos' by
wimmin.   Den de one wid de gaiters, he say, " You nig
tell de trute ; she *raal* cap'n ?   She bos' ebryting ? "   I
say, " Yas, saar-e !   ebryting !   She bos' steamboat.   She
bos' Pats.   She bos' Hank and me — Phus — dat's me
W'y !   mis' could bos' you, bos' de President 'nited States, be
cap'n ob ebrybody."   Den dey bof laf, an' I help' 'em obe
de gang-plank.

MARY (*sitting*). Oh, Phus! you tried to prove too much. But you make me laugh, in spite of my troubles.

PHUS. I does my bes', mis'. (*Sits down*, R., *and reads.*)

MR. R. The other owners say, and the newspapers, too, that you have no chance; and we are all so certain of it that we have agreed not to take away the boat if you do get the license.

MARY. Do you think yourselves so certain as that? Very well. But I have faith to believe that you will all wish that you had not made that promise, unless you really want me to have the boat.

MR. R. Oh, madam! we've no notion you'll get it. The other owners scorn the idea of a woman captain, and so do I. It's ridiculous! (*Walks about.*)

PHUS (*reading to himself*). W'ot did Meelissee scramded — no — squeemed for? 'coz she felt a col' han' on her fourhed? Golly! wos she 'f'aid o' dat? (*Reads*) Oh! she was alone in de dark, in de bed, an' couldn't see nobody! I should 'a' thought she would 'a' squeemed. (*Looks all around in a frightened manner.*)

MR. R. (*seating himself near* MARY). When did you hear from your husband last?

MARY. Not for a long time. I can't think what the reason is. I expected to find a letter here, but haven't received any. Phus!

PHUS (*jumping up in terror, and then relieved*). Oh! it's on'y mis'. Yaas! yaas!

MARY. Phus, you go to the post-office, and see if there are any letters. The post-man may not know that we have come in.

PHUS. Yaas, mis'. (*Puts book on the wheel-house, and exit* L.)

MR. R. He went out with a fishing-fleet, didn't he, from Gloucester?

MARY. Yes; why?

MR. R. Well, there have been a good many fishing-boats

lost lately, down at the Banks, that went from Gloucester.
What was the name of his boat?

MARY. The Betsey Ludgitt, Captain Zabulon Miller.

MR. R. That's the name of one of them, I think. Here's
the shipping list. It says (*he reads*), "Several vessels
strayed from the fleet, and have not been heard from since.
It is feared that they are lost. Among them is the Betsey
Ludgitt, Captain Zab — "

MARY (*rising in alarm*). Merciful Heaven! it cannot
be! I should have heard; something would have told me
if such a dreadful thing had happened to William. I cannot
believe it.

MR. R. He *may* be safe; but the probabilities are that
he is lost.

MARY. Oh! do not say that again. I cannot and will not
believe it. (*Goes to the hammock, and bends over it.*)

Mr. R. (*approaching* MARY *in an insinuating way*). My
dear — madam, if anything should happen to your husband,
remember (*smiling*) that you have a warm friend in me. I
will give you as good a home as there is on the river, and
take your child, too. Yes! yes! I'll take your child.

MARY (*turning suddenly upon him*). Give me a home?
Take my child? What do you mean?

MR. R. Why, I mean that I'll marry you!

MARY. Marry me? Who gave you the right to say
you'd marry me, or take my baby? William's child! How
dare you!

MR. R. I don't see as you can help yourself. You need
the protection of a man. You can't have the boat; and you
certainly can't get a living around here, with your hands tied
by that young one. And you're too pretty a woman —
(*Tries to take her hand.*)

MARY. (*indignantly*). Sir! you've said enough! You
may own my boat, and you may have the power to take her
from me; but you cannot have the wife of Captain William
Miller. I tell you, sir, that I would rather beg my way home
from door to door, with my child in my arms, — yes, I would

starve, — before I would be the wife of any man but my own husband. Dead or alive, it makes no difference to me. He is still my husband!

MR. R. (*aside*). Those down-East women beat the world. The spunk they show — Yankee grit they call it — it's amazing! But, Gad! it makes her look handsomer than ever. (*To her, insinuatingly*) You may change your mind ; but, whether you do or not, remember that I will always be your friend. (*Smiling.*)

MARY. Sir! I shall *never* change my mind ; and I forbid you ever to mention this subject to me again. I want no such friendship as yours. Good-morning! (*Turns from him, and goes to the hammock.*)

MR. R. (*apologetically*). Well, I'm sure I — (*Aside*) Gad! I want her more than ever. (*To her*) You know I said if you *did* get the license, we won't take away the boat. I'm sure you ought not to complain of that!

MARY (*without turning*). Very well, sir — then, there is nothing more to say. Good-morning.

MR. R. (*shamefacedly*). Er-er-good-morning. (*Exit R.*)

MARY (*scornfully*). So this is the way men *protect* women! Wretch! To dare to speak so to me!

(*Re-enter* PHUS, R.)

PHUS. O, mis'! dere's an ol' gemmen an' young maars on de warf, an' dey bof ax for you.

MARY. Why, who can they be? Ask them to come on deck.

PHUS (*at R.*). Dis way! Dis way!

(CAPTAIN GANDY, *outside, sings.*)

"On Springfield maount'ins there did dwell
A lovelye youth an' known full well — "

MARY (*in great surprise*). Father Gandy!

(*Enter* CAPT. G. *at R., with* J. Q. A., *in the uniform of a railroad-train boy, with a basket on his arm.*)

MARY. Why, father! Where *did* you come from? And

John Quincy Adams! (*Rushes into his arms, spilling the basket.*)

J. Q. A. Here! Here! What are you about, spilling all my spondulics! (*Puts down his basket, and takes off his hat.*)

MARY. Dear, dear father! where in the world did you come from? (*Throws her arms round him.*)

CAPT G. Why! from hum, o' coorse. Whar else should I hail from?

MARY (*eagerly*). Oh, father! do you know anything about William? I haven't heard from him for two months, and I can't think what the reason is. You don't suppose anything could have happened to him, do you?

CAPT. G. Oh! wal, no — I guess not. I saw by the *Herald* that Zab Miller's skewner had strayed from the rest on 'em; but he knows wot he's abaout. He ain't a-gwine ter tell all Glowchester where them skewls o' haulibaout hide. (*Pats her on the shoulder.*) Don't yer worry abaout that! There ain't no telegraph poles on them fishin' graounds, an' the postman don't drop in every day in them diggin's, an' there ain't no delivery if yer do write, nuther.

MARY. I can't help worrying; and yet I know he must be safe. But, father, how did *you* happen to come?

CAPT. G. Wal, yer marm was so worrited abaout your trouble that she made me start off; coz she sed I could act as cap'n, if that was all the gov'ment wanted, be "master in name" (she read it in the *Globe*), so's you could keep the boat. (*Shoves hat on back of head, puts hands in pockets, and walks about, sailor fashion.*)

J. Q. A. *I* was the first one to think of coming. And I went to Boston on Jim Rosson's engine, and got a chance as train-boy to New York. And when marm found out I was bound to come, she said pup should go, too. I wanted to come and punch old Romberg's head. (*Walks about and inspects everything.*)

MARY. But where did you get the money to come with, father? and, John (*to* J. Q. A.), who paid your fare from New York?

J. Q. A. Why! I paid myself, of course. What do you take me for? When I got to New York I got another chance as train-boy, all the way through; and I've peddled out water in a big-nosed coffee-pot from Annisport to New Orleans. And sold books, too! And prize packages, and things, and magazines. (*Calls*) "Harper's! December Harper's! Baby Pathfinder! Puck! Peanuts! Gum drops? (*Offers his basket to* MARY.)

MARY. You funny boy!

CAPT. G. Well, yer see, yer marm —

MARY (*interrupting*). Sit down, father. (*Offers him a camp-stool.*)

CAPT. G. No, I just 's lives stand. (*Leans against railing.*) Yer marm took boarders all summer, an' she made me take that money. She said 'twould never do any more good; an', then, Leafy Jane, she's l'arnt the millinger's trade, an' she giv' me some o' hern.

J. Q. A. I tried to get a pass for him, part way, at least; but them railroad men are so mean they'll never help a fellow along.

CAPT. G. Haow is little Nate?

MARY. Oh! he's all right! Here he is, father. Come and see him. (*They go together to the hammock.*) He hasn't been sick a day this summer. The dear little fellow! He grows like a weed.

J. Q. A. (*at the hammock, aside*). A pig weed, I s'pose.

CAPT. G. Yer see, Mary, yer trouble has set me ter thinkin'; an' when you wrote they was goin' to take away yer boat, just cos yer was a woman, by the great horn spoon, I was mad: for yer a Gandy cl'ar through, a sea-cap'n born like all the rest on us. And I've made up my mind that wimmin's rights must be worth suthin' to wimmin, as well as men's rights to men. An', as old Pete Rosson said, when he felt so bad about yer losing the boat, "Sence a woman can't allus hev her husband or her father tew take care on her, she ort to have the right to take care o' herself, an' then she can use

it or not, as she wants tew." An' so I begin to think that I
don't care if we do let 'em vote.

J. Q. A. (*examining the wheel*). Cracky! you can't
make me believe that. I shall vote in five years, and I'm
sure I don't want Leafy Jane taggin' after me to the poles.
'Tain't any place for girls.

CAPT. G. Stop yer gab! Wait till yer ten year older
an' then if yer up for *see*-lectman, yer'll be glad enuf ter have
'em vote for *yaou!*

J. Q. A. Wouldn't I make a healthy selectman? Yes, I
guess not!

CAPT. G. An' — an', Mary, I want to tell yer suthin' else.
I gin in about yer mother's caarf, an' went an' bought
her back. To be sure, she ain't a caarf no longer, but a good
likely heifer; but yer mother sez the principle 's just as
good as if she was jest born, or as old as Methuselum. An'
she's tickled enuf abaout it, an' she said men ain't so bad
arter all, if yer can onny make 'em see what is wimmin's jest
dues.

(*Enter* PHUS, L.)

PHUS. Oh, mis'! dere's a s'prise for yer, a golly big one!

MARY. A surprise! What is it?

PHUS. Dere's two ladies talking to Hank; an' one looks
so peart, so peart, oh, Lor'! (*Turns to* R. *Aside*) I wan'
tell her de res'. O, golly! I can't keep in.

MARY. Talking to Hank? Some of his lady friends, I
suppose.

PHUS. O, yes! I forgets. Dey wants ter see you, dey
say, and Hank say he bring'd 'em in.

(*Enter* HANK, R., *in a stage sailor suit, with* MRS.
GANDY *and* LEAFY JANE, *the latter very stylishly dressed.*)

MARY. Mother! Leafy Jane! (*Rushes to them.*) Well,
this *is* a surprise, I should think.

CAPT. G. (*in great surprise*). I vum to vummy, I am
beat now!

PHUS. Wot I tole yer? Wot I tol yer, mis'? (*Aside.*)
But de odder one's bigger!

CAPT. G.   Waal, I swan to man, Lorany! you've got ahead on us this time.   (*Goes up to her*)   Tarnation! haow glad I am ter see yer!

MARY.   Why, Leafy Jane, how you've grown!

J. Q. A.   Yes, and she feels bigger'n you do, and puts on a plaguy sight more airs.   She wants father (she calls him par) to put an *e* in Gandy, 'cause she says it's more genteel. — And say! she don't lithp (*lisp*) any more; the customers laughed at her so for saying "yeth, thir."

CAPT. G. (*to* MRS. G.).   Where *in* the world 'd you come from?

MRS. G. (*deliberately sitting, and removing bonnet, mitts, etc.*).   Waal, Nathan, we heerd of an exertion train daown here, at redooced rates; an' the boarders, — one on 'em's writin' a book, — an' wanted to be quiet, — said they'd take the haouse furnished for tew months, and pay in advance. And so Leafy an' me come right along.   She's made a lot o' bunnits this fall on her own accaount, so she's quite a haruss (*heiress*).

L. J.   Oh, mar!

MRS. G.   Yer see, par, we hadn't time to write after we'd made up our mind to start, an' we cum a leetle sooner'n we should ef it hadn't 'a' been for comin' with — er — with —

L. J. (*whispers warningly*).   Why, mar!

MRS. G. — with the exertionists. (*Aside*).   Why *in* the world don't he come?   I'm tired o' keepin' it in.   He said he onny wanted to go ter the bank.   (*To* MARY)   An' then I was afraid you or the baby — why! where *is* the baby?   Do les see him!

MARY.   He's asleep, mother.   Here, come and see him. Isn't he a darling?   (*They go to the hammock.*)

L. J.   Oh, Mary, what made you name the baby Nathan? I wish you had called him Herbert, Ernest, or Montmorenci. It's so much more genteel.

J. Q. A.   Montmorenci Miller!   Cracky! wouldn't that be tony?

L. J. (*scornfully*). Tony! (*Walks off with* HANK *to the wheel-house.*)

MRS. G. (*To* MARY) We tole yer young man that looks so much like Fred Douglass not to tell yer who we was.

J. Q. A. Marm won't say " colored man."

MRS. G. No, I won't; I'm sick o' readin' on't in the newspapers. They're allus sayin' such a man, *colored*, had his leg took off, or died, or suthin'. What difference does it make, I should like to know, whether he's colored or not! He's hurt all the same, ain't he? an' he's a man, tew, all the same, ain't he?

PHUS (*aside*). Golly! I shall bust!

MARY (*to* MRS. G.). How long can you stay? a good while, I hope.

HANK (*steps forward, drawls*). I think we must start in about three weeks from Monday, if all the signs come right. (*To* MARY) You see the excursion don't last only till then.

MARY (*in surprise*). We must start! What in the world does this mean?

HANK. Wal, you see, Leafy and me, we've been a-writin' back and forth sence the cap'n told me I'd better; an' she's agreed to hev me, an' go an' live down to Nantucket. Grandfather's old, and my marm wants me to come home an' settle down an' see to things. She says she's tired o' housekeeping, and wants to see some young folks round.

J. Q. A. (*to* L. J.). 'Fore I'd marry a cook! Anybody that feels as big as you do. Cookie Mudgitt! How are you, Mrs. Cookie Mudgitt!

CAPT. G. Hold your yorp! Hundreds of big men hev ben cooks. There was the most worshipful G. M. of aour Masonic Lodge, he used to be cook in Annisport Jail, an' now he's a 'surance man, an' lives in a tarnal big haouse. An', then, there was a feller cooked on a ranch five year', an' they sent him to Congress.

MARY. Oh, Hank! what shall we do without you?

HANK. I tho't o' that. But a nice French Creole feller

is takin' my place to-day ; an' if he does well, p'r'aps you'll
keep him. If not, I'll find somebody else afore we go.

MARY (*to* L. J.). When are you going to be married ?

L. J. (*loftily*). As soon as we have made the needed
preparations. Henry will explain.

J. Q. A. (*to* HANK). Then, that's what you're so
rigged up for, ain't it, Bub ? in all them sailor slops. You
look like a royal tar, a regular old Britisher.

HANK (*sheepishly*). ·Why, yes ; you see, Leafy, she likes
it. But as soon as the weddin' is over (she wants me to be
married in 'em here on the boat), I mean to put the whole
rig away in my sea-chist, with them blasted books that de-
luded me into goin' to sea; an' that will be the last of my
bein' a sailor. I've had enough of it. Darn the bunks! I
want to sleep on a first-rate feather-bed the rest of my life.

L. J. Law! Henry. How you do talk!

HANK. It's a fact, Leafy, so there ! (*He goes up to her
and tries to kiss her.*)

L. J. (*pushing him away*). There ! that will do, Henry.
That's seven times to-day since I came.

HANK. Is it ? Well, 'tain't any too many, anyhow !

J. Q. A. You great galloot ! Catch me ever being such a
fool. Say! what kind of a necktie you going to wear ?

HANK. Oh, a stunner! blue and yallar, I guess. (*Looks
at* L. J.) Sha'n't I, Leafy ?

L. J. (*with dignity*). No, Henry ; you must have one to
match my dress.

J. Q. A. (*to* L. J.). 'Fore I'd go taggin' 'way down to New
Orleans after a husband !

L. J. You'll have to tag all round the world before you'll
find any one fool enough to wed *you.*

J. Q. A. I don't think I shall ever "wed." My affections
have been blighted by a fair damsel from Chicago. She had
large feet.

MRS. G. Stop, John Quincy! Yer as sarsy daown
here as yer was ter hum ; ain't ye l'arnt nothin' by
travellin' ?

(PHUS, *who has been examining* J. Q. A.'s *basket, attracted by the peanuts, puts his hand in his pocket for money to buy some, and, feeling a letter there, draws it forth.*)

PHUS. Golly, I forgets dat let'! Mis'! mis'! here's a let'; seems it mus' be dat licens'. Yes! see dis great t'ing on it, big as a hoe-cake and red as a 'simmon.

MARY (*eagerly*). Give it to me! (*Breaks the seal and hastily reads.*)

NEW ORLEANS, Feb. 8, 1884.

MRS. MARY MILLER: Dear madam, I take great pleasure in forwarding to you a captain's license, for a Mississippi steamboat, granted according to the decision of Secretary Folger, under Section 4439 of the Revised Statutes of the United States.

Very Respectfully,

DANIEL DUMONT.

Supervising Inspector-General.

(MARY *bursts into tears, and sits down.*)

PHUS. Is it, mis'? Is it de licens'?

MARY (*rising proudly, and holding it out*). Yes, it is my license; and I am Captain Mary Miller! (*Hands paper to* CAPT. G.)

HANK. Hurrah! Three cheers for Captain Mary Miller!

J. Q. A. And a Tiger-r-r-rrr!

(PATSY *looks in, then enters and listens*).

CAPT. G. I thought Charles J. Folger 'd hev the rights on't.

MRS. G. Them Folgers could allus be depended on to do the right thing; believed in ekality from the beginnin'. Old Ben Franklin was one on 'em, and Lucreshy Mott. They ain't a bit like some o' them Nantucket Halletts — allus on the wrong side of ekality.

PHUS. Lor' bress Cap'n Mary Miller, cap'n of de Keyhole's Bride. (*Seizes his banjo, sings uproariously, and dances about.*)

Bress de men at Washington, — 'Lijah cum down.
Dat made a woman cap'n, — 'Lijah cum down.

But bress above dem all, — 'Lijah cum down.

Good Seketelly Folger, — 'Lijah cum down.

May de charyott ob Erlijah swing him softly up to
(*Slower*)   Heben,

An' Mary Miller's blessin' be his eberlastin' crown.

MRS. G. (*to him, aside*). You go'n see ef he ain't a-comin'.
I can't hold in much longer. (*Exit* PHUS, R.)

PATSY. Faix, mum, I'll shthay wid ye as lang as ye varnt.

MARY. But, Patsy, if you do stay, you must expect to
obey orders.

PATSY. For sure, mum ; I shpects to 'bey a raal lay-
censed cap'n. (*Goes to wheel and sits by it.*)

MARY. And now I am captain of my own vessel in name
as well as in reality. God bless Secretary Folger! He has
saved us from want, protected our little home, and given a
woman the right to be captain of her own boat. If William
were only here!

PHUS (*entering in great excitement*). Oh, mis'! here's de
biggest s'prise in de worl'! (*Beckoning.*) Dis way! Dis way!

(*Enter* CAPTAIN MILLER, L. *All rise.*)

CAPT. M. Mary!

MARY. My dear William! I knew you would come
back! (*Embraces him.*)

CAPT. M. Of course, my darling wife. Why shouldn't I
come back?

MARY. Why, the papers said your vessel had drifted from
the rest, and —

CAPT. M. That is true. But we drifted to some purpose,
for we struck a splendid school of halibut, and we stayed
till we filled up. That's the reason I did not write.
And when we landed, I ran up to Annisport, and found
Mother Gandy and Leafy Jane wanted to come with me, and
so we all came along together.

(*Shakes hands all round, returns to* MARY.)

MARY. But, William, where have you been all this time?

CAPT. M. Oh, I had to go to the bank for father to pay
the interest on a note —

MRS. G.   But we thought we'd come right along —

MARY.   Why didn't you tell me, mother?

MRS. G.   William told me not to.   He wanted to s'prise yer.

J. Q. A.   She thought she wouldn't "tell you all at once, for fear you couldn't bore it."

PHUS.   I seen de cap'n at de pos'-office.   He say, "How Mis Miller?"   I say, "Bos', an' de baby, too."   Golly, wa'n't it a big s'prise?

MARY.   See, William, here's my license as captain.   I sent to Washington for a license, and here it is.   (*Shows it to him.*)

MRS. G.   Think of aour Mary's bein' a cap'n.   Haow lucky!   An', naow, if anything happens to you, William, she can allus get a livin', 'cos she can manage her own boat.

J. Q. A.   Yes, and she can paddle her own canoe.

L. J.   John Quincy Adams Gandy, how very vulgar!

CAPT. G. (*to* WILLIAM).   What'll *you* do, neaow Mary's made capt'n?   Haow'll *you* git along?

MARY.   Oh, we'll both be captains.

CAPT. M.   No!   She shall be captain still; and I'll be her mate.   It won't be the first time a man has sailed through life under the orders of a brave and true-hearted woman, — nor the last, I hope.   And so, Captain Mary Miller, I salute you.   (*Makes a naval salute.*)

PHUS.   Wid a kiss!   wid a kiss!   Mars cap'n, kiss mis' cap'n.

CAPT. M.   Yes, to please you, my good fellow (and myself also), it shall be with a kiss.   (*Kisses her hand*).   My captain!

Disposition of characters:

R.	C.	L.
CAPT. G. MRS. G.		HANK AND L. J.

CAPT. M. AND MARY.

J. Q. A.   PHUS.